A NATION IS BORN:
WORLD WAR I AND INDEPENDENCE
1910-1929

TITLE LIST

Before Canada: First Nations and First Contacts, Prehistory–1523

The Settlement of New France and Acadia, 1524–1701

Britain's Canada, 1613–1770

Conflicts, Changes, and Confederation, 1770–1867

From the Atlantic to the Pacific: Canadian Expansion, 1867–1909

A Nation Is Born: World War I and Independence, 1910–1929

Crisis at Home and Abroad:
The Great Depression, World War II, and Beyond, 1929–1959

Redefining Canada: A Developing Identity, 1960–1984

Canada's Changing Society, 1984–the Present

Canada's Modern-Day First Nations:
Nunavut and Evolving Relationships

A NATION IS BORN:
WORLD WAR I AND INDEPENDENCE
1910-1929

BY
SHEILA NELSON

MASON CREST PUBLISHERS
PHILADELPHIA

Mason Crest Publishers Inc.
370 Reed Road
Broomall, Pennsylvania 19008
(866) MCP-BOOK (toll free)

First printing
1 2 3 4 5 6 7 8 9 10

Library of Congress Cataloging-in-Publication Data

Nelson, Sheila.
  A nation is born : World War I and independence, 1910–1929 / by Sheila Nelson.
     p. cm. — (How Canada became Canada)
  Includes index.
  ISBN 1-4222-0006-X   ISBN 1-4222-0000-0 (series)
  1. Canada—History—1914–1945—Juvenile literature. 2. Canada—Politics and government—1914–1945—Juvenile literature. 3. Nationalism—Canada—History—20th century—Juvenile literature. 4. World War, 1914–1918—Canada—Juvenile literature. 5. World War, 1914–1918—Participation, Canadian—Juvenile literature. 6. Great Britain—Colonies—Administration—History—20th century—Juvenile literature. I. Title.
  F1034.N29 2006
  971.062—dc22
                              2005011620

Produced by Harding House Publishing Service, Inc.
www.hardinghousepages.com
Interior design by MK Bassett-Harvey.
Cover design by Dianne Hodack.
Printed in the Hashemite Kingdom of Jordan.

CONTENTS

Introduction   6
1. Questions of Nationalism   9
2. Canada and the Great War   23
3. The War at Home   41
4. Toward a Greater Independence   57
5. The Need for Social Freedom   65
Time Line   78
Further Reading   82
For More Information   83
Index   84
Picture Credits   86
Biographies   87

INTRODUCTION

by David Bercuson

Every country's history is distinct, and so is Canada's. Although Canada is often said to be a pale imitation of the United States, it has a unique history that has created a modern North American nation on its own path to democracy and social justice. This series explains how that happened.

Canada's history is rooted in its climate, its geography, and in its separate political development. Virtually all of Canada experiences long, dark, and very cold winters with copious amounts of snowfall. Canada also spans several distinct geographic regions, from the rugged western mountain ranges on the Pacific coast to the forested lowlands of the St. Lawrence River Valley and the Atlantic tidewater region.

Canada's regional divisions were complicated by the British conquest of New France at the end of the Seven Years' War in 1763. Although Britain defeated France, the French were far more numerous in Canada than the British. Britain was thus forced to recognize French Canadian rights to their own language, religion, and culture. That recognition is now enshrined in the Canadian Constitution. It has made Canada a democracy that values group rights alongside individual rights, with official French/English bilingualism as a key part of the Canadian character.

During the American Revolution, Canadians chose to stay British. After the Revolution, they provided refuge to tens of thousands of Americans who, for one reason or another, did not follow George Washington, Benjamin Franklin, or the other founders of the United States who broke with Britain.

Democracy in Canada under the British Crown evolved more slowly than it did in the United States. But in the early nineteenth century, slavery was outlawed in the

British Empire, and as a result, also in Canada. Thus Canada never experienced civil war or government-imposed racial segregation.

From these few, brief examples, it is clear that Canada's history differs considerably from that of the United States. And yet today, Canada is a true North American democracy in its own right. Canadians will profit from a better understanding of how their country was shaped—and Americans may learn much about their own country by studying the story of Canada.

The faraway land of
South Africa played
a major role in
Canadian identity.

One
QUESTIONS OF NATIONALISM

Far away, in South Africa, war was brewing between British settlers and the Dutch Boers. In Canada, the issue stirred up heated debates across the country.

"Of course we will send Canadian troops to South Africa to help the British!" exclaimed the imperialists. "We are British, too!"

"How dare Britain assume Canada will support her little colonial war!" protested the nationalists. "Canada is an independent country! We should make our own decisions, and we should decide not to send troops to South Africa!"

In 1867, Britain had passed the British North America Act, creating the country of Canada. Although the act gave Canada the power to govern its own affairs within the country, the British monarch still had the ultimate control, especially when dealing with questions of international importance.

Sir Wilfrid Laurier became prime minister of Canada in 1896. While British politicians pushed for closer ties between Britain and Canada in terms of trade and military support, Laurier focused instead on developing Canada as a country.

A soldier in the British army during the Boer War

British troops in South Africa during the Boer War

The Boer War

The Boer War of 1899 was a conflict fought between the Boers—white South Africans descended from earlier Dutch settlers—and more recent British arrivals. Sparked by the discovery of gold in South Africa, the Boer War was the first major conflict Britain had become involved with since the British North America Act of 1867. Britain assumed

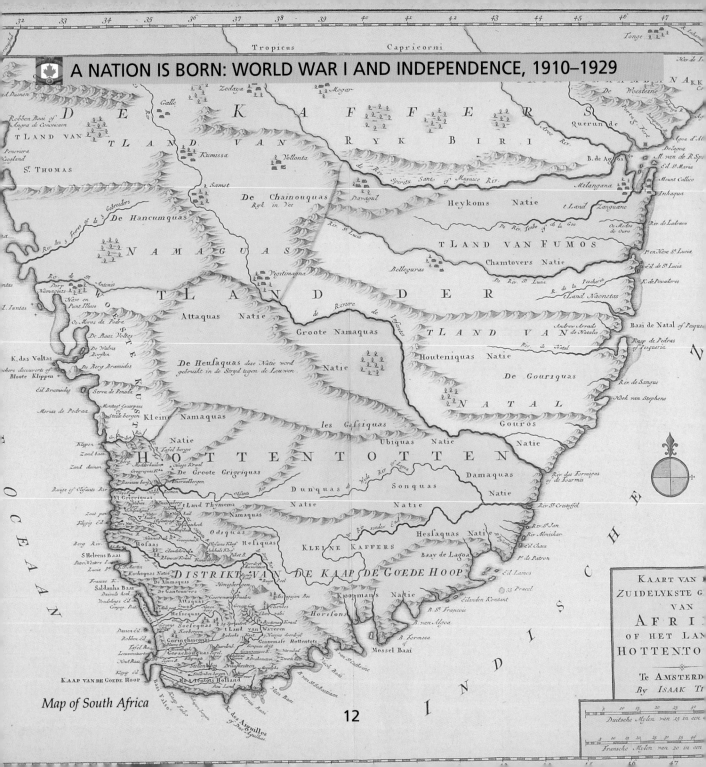

Map of South Africa

Canada, as a member of the British Empire, would naturally send troops to fight on the side of Britain in South Africa.

Some Canadians wanted to send soldiers to support the British. They felt this was the only real option. These people were the imperialists, those who believed Canada's position as a member of the British Empire was just as important—if not more important—than Canada's status as an independent country.

The nationalists, on the other hand, thought Canada should be able to function independently from Britain, making decisions to benefit Canada rather than Britain. These people did not want to send troops to South Africa. Many French Canadians were nationalists; their heritage was French, not British. They did not care very much about taking care of the British Empire; their focus was on building up Canada itself. What's more, some French Canadians, looking at the situation in South Africa, sympathized with the Boers. Over a hundred years earlier, in 1763, Britain had conquered New France, and now Britain wanted to conquer the Boers.

With the imperialists clamoring on one side and the nationalists on the other, Prime Minister Laurier was torn. He was a French Canadian, and he agreed with the nationalists that the Boer War really did not have anything to do with Canada—but he wanted to satisfy as many Canadians as possible.

Laurier came up with a compromise. Canada would send a volunteer force to South Africa to support the British. Only those who wanted to fight needed to go. Britain would pay the Canadian soldiers and take total responsibility for them while they were in South Africa.

Volunteers were not difficult to find; many young English Canadian men were eager to fight for Britain. Nearly eight thousand Canadian soldiers, along with twelve nurses, traveled to South Africa.

Neither the imperialists nor the nationalists were entirely happy with Laurier's compromise. The imperialists thought Canada should do more. They wanted to send more troops and send them more officially. Laurier's decision to let Britain pay and maintain the Canadian soldiers did not satisfy the imperialists.

The nationalists thought Laurier had gone too far by sending any troops at all to South Africa. One Member of Parliament in particular, Henri Bourassa, spoke out against Laurier. Although Bourassa had supported Laurier at one time, he now condemned him for "selling out" to the imperialists. In 1899, he resigned from the House of Commons in disgust over Canada's participation in the Boer War, but he was reelected almost immediately. Bourassa would continue to speak for the nationalists over the next decades, fighting to keep Canada independent from the influence of Britain.

A Canadian Navy

The Boer War ended in 1902 with the surrender of the Boers, and South Africa became part of the British Empire. Almost immediately, Britain began to concentrate on strengthening the empire, urging Laurier to commit Canada to closer ties with Britain.

Britain had long wanted Canada to contribute to the British navy, but Laurier had refused. Now, the British were becoming nervous as they watched Germany build its military. In 1909, Britain held an Imperial Defence Conference with the countries of the British Empire. Britain wanted their support against any possible German threat, and it especially wanted help building its naval strength.

Imperialists in Canada wanted to contribute to the British navy, but nationalists

The First Ships

The first two ships in the Canadian navy were the HMCS *Niobe* and the HMCS *Rainbow*, both cruisers. (HMCS stood for His Majesty's Canadian Ships.) Both were built by the British navy and used for several years before being transferred to Canada. The *Niobe* made port in Halifax, Nova Scotia, and the *Rainbow* patrolled the fishing grounds of coastal British Columbia.

The CGS Canada, *one of the first ships in the Royal Canadian Navy*

were against the idea. The nationalists liked the idea of a Canadian navy, but they wanted it to be completely under Canada's control. Again, Laurier saw the opportunity for compromise between the opposing groups. Instead of contributing to Britain's navy, Canada would build its own, but if Britain ever entered another war, Laurier guaranteed the British government that the Canadian naval force would be available to support the British.

Bourassa and the nationalists were not pleased with this compromise either. They did not feel it was a compromise at all, but gave the imperialists exactly what they wanted—closer ties with Britain and a promise of Canadian support in case of war. With the growing tensions between Britain and Germany, the likelihood of Canada being pulled into a war seemed likely.

The Naval Service of Canada was officially created on May 4, 1910. The fleet consisted of five cruisers and six destroyers and would be staffed by a volunteer force. In 1911, its name was changed to the Royal Canadian Navy.

Today, Laurier's face appears on the Canadian five-dollar bill.

Annexation means taking possession of a territory.

The Election of 1911

Sir Wilfrid Laurier had been prime minister of Canada for fifteen years at the time of the general election in September of 1911. He had lost many supporters with the creation of the Canadian navy. During his 1911 campaign, Laurier introduced another issue as well—free trade with the United States. Canadians had never trusted the idea of opening up trade with the United States. They feared the possibility of American *annexation* and felt free trade harmed Canadian businesses and manufacturers.

In 1910, Laurier had traveled to the western provinces. There, he had learned how the farmers wanted free trade so they would not have to transport their grain back east to

How Is a Prime Minister Chosen?

In Canada, a general election does not directly elect the prime minister. Instead, each voting district (called "ridings") elects a representative to Parliament. The leader of the party that gets the most parliamentary seats then becomes prime minister.

Canada's farmland

sell and so they would be able to buy farm equipment from just over the border in the United States. To help these farmers and to gain western support, Laurier promised during his election campaign to introduce a limited form of free trade, one intended to help western Canadian farmers without hurting Canadian manufacturers.

Throughout Canada's history, various Liberal candidates had tried to run for election on a platform of free trade. None of these candidates had ever become prime

Robert Borden

minister. Most Canadians preferred the Conservative Party's high *tariffs* that protected Canada's businesses. When Laurier, a Liberal, won the election of 1896, he had done so by abandoning the Liberal idea of free trade. In 1911, he trusted that his base of western support for free trade would be enough to win him the election.

Although the Liberals did win the majority of seats in Saskatchewan and Alberta, this was not enough. Québec traditionally voted Liberal, and while Laurier did retain a slight majority there, he had lost much of his support with the creation of the Canadian navy. Ontario had the highest number of seats, and most of them went to the Conservatives. On October 10, 1911, Sir Wilfrid Laurier stepped down, and Robert Borden of the Conservative Party became prime minister of Canada.

Throughout the Laurier years, Canada had faced difficult questions about its relationship with Great Britain. The imperialists and the nationalists disagreed intensely about the nature of this relationship, whether Canada should have more or less involvement with British affairs. Laurier had chosen to make compromises to try and appease both groups. While these compromises really did not make either group happy at the time, Laurier is remembered today as a great nation builder.

The conflict between the imperialists and the nationalists brought about by the Boer War and the Canadian navy was only a prelude to the coming dispute over Canada's role in World War I. The countries of Europe simmered with hostilities and alliances. Soon, the continent would erupt in the worst war the world had ever seen. An ocean away, Canada, bound by ties with Britain, could not remain unaffected.

Tariffs are duties or taxes a government places on imported or exported goods.

Troops during World War I

Two

CANADA AND THE GREAT WAR

On a sunny morning in June of 1914, a motorcade carrying Archduke Franz Ferdinand, heir to the throne of Austria-Hungary, and his wife, Sophie, rolled through the streets of Sarajevo. Sarajevo was a part of the Austro-Hungarian Empire at this time, but many from the nearby country of Serbia believed all the Slavic areas of the empire should become part of Serbia. As the cars rolled slowly through the crowded streets, a young man stepped out suddenly and threw a bomb directly at the archduke's car.

At first, no one was sure what had happened. The bomb hit the side of the car and bounced off, rolling toward the car behind. The explosion shook the street. People screamed and ran. The driver of the archduke's car sped up, whisking his passengers away to their planned reception at City Hall.

The archduke and his wife were shaken, but unhurt. "No one would try to kill me twice in one day," he said, but at the mayor's urging, he agreed to leave the city as quickly and quietly as possible.

On a small side street, the archduke's car slowed to make a tight turn. Gavril Princip, a nineteen-year-old Serbian revolutionary, ran suddenly at the car, firing his gun at the archduke and his wife, shooting and killing them both.

Basic training is the initial military training of recruits.

Canada Goes to War

Before long, the news of the archduke's assassination reached Canada. People thought the incident was shocking and tragic, but they never suspected it would set off an international war. A month after the shooting—following a halfhearted attempt at diplomatic negotiations—Austria-Hungary declared war on Serbia.

This declaration of war did not simply affect Austria-Hungary and Serbia. Europe in the early twentieth century was a tangle of complex alliances. Russia had promised to protect Serbia in case of war and immediately began mobilizing its army. Germany, allied with Austria-Hungary, tried to quickly conquer France—an ally of Russia—before the Russian army could move far. Germany did not want to fight a war to both its east and its west, so it launched an attack on France by avoiding the fortified border between France and Germany and instead marching through the neutral country of Belgium. France had already started getting its troops ready to support Russia. In response to the invasion of Belgium, Great Britain declared war on Germany to protect its ally. With Britain's declaration of war, Canada was automatically at war as well.

This was no Boer War. With Britain and France both fighting on the same side in Europe, both English Canadians and French Canadians had reason to support their mother countries. Canadians were eager to go to war. Thousands of young Canadians gathered near Québec City at Valcartier Camp for *basic training*. In October of 1914, the Canadian Expeditionary Force of 32,000 men left Canada in a convoy of ships bound for Great Britain.

In the same convoy traveled five hundred men from the Newfoundland Regiment, made up of volunteers from across

Archduke Franz Ferdinand

Soldiers after one of the Ypres battles

In Flanders Fields

In May of 1915, Major John McCrae, a Canadian military doctor, stood over the fresh grave of his young friend Lieutenant Alexis Helmer, killed by a shell during the Second Battle of Ypres. As he mourned, he began to compose the first lines of what would become the most popular poem of the First World War.

In Flanders fields the poppies blow
Between the crosses, row on row,
That mark our place; and in the sky
The larks, still bravely singing, fly
Scarce heard amid the guns below.

We are the Dead. Short days ago
We lived, felt dawn, saw sunset glow,
Loved and were loved, and now we lie
    In Flanders fields.

Take up our quarrel with the foe:
To you with failing hands we throw
The torch; be yours to hold it high.
If ye break faith with us who die
We shall not sleep, though poppies grow
    In Flanders fields

France's poppies

the island—then a self-governing colony. In Britain, the Canadians and the New-foundlanders faced more training before the British decided they were ready for the battlefields of France. They were eager to begin fighting, cheerfully and enthusiastically believing the war would quickly be won.

Ypres

The first major battle Canadian forces took part in was the Second Battle of Ypres, beginning at the end of April in 1915. The previous autumn, British forces had driven back the Germans at Ypres, a small Belgian town not far from the English Channel, and had managed to hold the town since then. On April 22, however, Germany introduced a new weapon.

Men looked up at clouds of yellow gas blowing toward them. Men ran for their lives, coughing and choking, but thousands of French and Algerian soldiers died in the trenches along the front line as the poisonous chlorine gas billowed over them. The line held by the Allied forces broke, leaving a four-mile (7-kilometer) gap unprotected. The Germans had not expected their attack to be so successful, and fortunately for the Allies, they did not have troops ready to take advantage of the breach. The newly ar-

rived Canadian soldiers were to hold the line and keep the Germans from advancing.

The use of poison gas during warfare had been outlawed—along with aerial bombardment—at the Hague Convention of 1899, but the Germans had used it anyway. The Allies scrambled to find a defense against the chemical weapon and to manufacture their own chlorine gas.

For the next month, Canadian and British forces tried to push the Germans back from Ypres, enduring repeated shelling and chlorine gas attacks. Breathing through handkerchiefs soaked in their own urine—a primitive form of gas mask—the Canadians fought through the gas.

By the end of May, the battle was over, ending only when ammunition began to run out. No real ground had been gained by either side. The only thing different was that now the Allies knew they faced poisonous gas attacks. And more than 100,000 men were dead: 35,000 Germans and 68,000 Allied forces.

The Battle of the Somme

The next year, Canadians found themselves in an even worse battle. Though the Battle of the Somme was a long and costly four-and-

The Ypres battlefield

Members of the Newfoundland Regiment

No-Man's-Land was the unoccupied area between opposing forces during the world wars.

a-half-month fight along the Somme River in northern France, it is usually remembered for its first day. On July 1, 1916, at seven-thirty in the morning, the attack began. For a week, the Allies had been bombarding the German lines. Most of the soldiers were cheerful and optimistic, believing that nearly all the Germans would be killed in this bombardment, and they would only need to finish the job. They were confident the battle would soon be over.

Things went wrong almost immediately. At Beaumont Hamel, the First Newfoundland Regiment struck out across *No-Man's-Land*, ordered to secure the first lines of German

Graves of men who lost their lives at the Somme

trenches. Artillery fire from the Allied trenches was to cover the advancing troops, but, because of a miscommunication, the Newfoundlanders were left unprotected. Most of the Germans had survived the bombardment of the past week, protected deep within their fortifications.

Machine guns rattled. More and more men fell as the Newfoundland Regiment reached the halfway point between the Allied and German lines. Men bent their heads against the hail of bullets as their companions collapsed dying and wounded around them. The few who reached the barbed wire in front of the German trenches found it hadn't been cut as they had been told. Men died tangled in wire. The next morning, only 68 of 790 men answered roll call in the Allied trenches; the rest were dead or wounded. Newfoundland had lost almost all of its fighting men in one day.

In the first day of the Battle of the Somme, the Allies suffered over 64,000 casualties, the worst one-day loss in the war. The battle dragged on for months, with neither side making any progress. The soldiers lived in a kind of nightmare. Above them, shells exploded, raining shrapnel down on their heads. Outside the trenches, the grass had been churned into a sea of gray mud, the trees blasted into jagged stumps. Within the trenches, the men were wet and miserable. Soldiers needed to keep their feet warm and dry, so they changed their socks several times a day; those whose feet got damp anyway suffered trench foot, which could quickly lead to gangrene and amputation.

In September, the British introduced the first tanks at the Somme. Tanks were heavily armored and could roll over barbed wire without difficulty. German bullets ricocheted harmlessly off the sides of the tanks, although artillery shells could still destroy them. Despite the success of their armor, the tanks were mechanically unreliable and could be caught on large pieces of debris. Tanks at the front broke down often, were snagged on broken tree trunks, and tipped into muddy craters.

By the time the Battle of the Somme ended in November, over 600,000 Allied soldiers had been killed or wounded. The Germans had lost nearly as many. The battle had no clear winner as both sides had lost much and gained very little. In all, it was one of the worst battles of the war.

Vimy Ridge

The long and terrible Battle of the Somme had taken its toll on the Allied soldiers. They had entered the war two years before with high spirits, optimistic, confident, and brimming with patriotic enthusiasm. By the beginning of 1917, most soldiers did not care anymore. Their patriotism and confidence had been eroded as the war dragged on and on. They wanted to go home. They wanted the war to end, whoever won. The Canadian soldiers, faced with day after day of mud and death, experienced the same feelings of depression.

Then, in April of 1917, the Canadian Expeditionary Force was assigned the task of capturing Vimy Ridge from the Germans. This was the first time during the war all four Canadian divisions fought together.

The Battle of Vimy Ridge became the defining battle of the First World War for Canada. Vimy Ridge was one of the most strongly fortified areas of the German line. The ridge was honeycombed with tunnels,

A Canadian soldier in World War I

crowned with rolls of barbed wire, and a small railway provided the Germans with a constant stream of fresh supplies. Capturing Vimy Ridge seemed like a nearly impossible task for the Canadian Expeditionary Force.

The Canadians planned their attack carefully. For a week, they bombarded the Germans heavily to wear them down. On the morning of April 9, the day after Easter, they launched their main attack.

The Canadians crept across No-Man's-Land, just behind a protective curtain of artillery fire. The approach had to be timed exactly right or the soldiers would be caught in their own artillery attack. The well-planned strike succeeded; by afternoon, the Canadians had captured the ridge, and in the next few days they would secure Vimy Ridge and their victory.

The capture of Vimy Ridge had been costly for the Canadians, their victory hard won, like most of the battles of the First World War. They had suffered over ten thousand casualties during the four days of the battle; over a third of those had been killed. The Germans lost twice as many.

Vimy Ridge was a small battle in a large war. It was part of the larger Battle of Arras, which lasted for five weeks and ended in a near stalemate. For the Canadians, however, it was a triumph of nationhood. Men from every part of Canada had come together and succeeded—without the help of Britain. In fact, the Battle of Vimy Ridge was one of the best organized of the war. A year later, the Allies still controlled Vimy Ridge and were able to use the location to strike at the heart of German territory. Canadians felt the elation of victory, and Britain looked at them with new respect.

The Canadians at Passchendaele

Passchendaele

With their victory at Vimy Ridge, the Canadians had earned a reputation as an elite fighting force. In October of 1917, the British ordered two of the Canadian divisions to recapture the Belgian village of Passchendaele, near Ypres. The Allies had been trying to take Passchendaele since the end of July, without success.

In July, the Germans had introduced a new chemical weapon: mustard gas. Unlike chlorine gas, which was deadly but against which the Allies' gas masks now protected them, mustard gas was not intended to kill—and gas masks were no use against it.

In the wake of the Battle of Passchendaele

*To **incapacitate** means to make powerless or ineffective.*

***Decimation** means wide-spread destruction.*

Protective covering worn by World War I soldiers facing mustard gas

The oily yellow vapor soaked through clothing and burned into skin. Skin blistered when it came into contact with the gas, and eyes went blind, either temporarily or permanently, depending on the length of exposure. The Germans intended the mustard gas to slow down the enemy and ***incapacitate*** them. Wounded men needed to be rescued; dead men did not.

The battlefield was an ocean of mud, a wet marsh where wounded men drowned facedown. In November, the Canadians captured Passchendaele, but at a cost of nearly sixteen thousand men. The fighting had nearly completely destroyed the village itself. To most, the battle had been pointless. The gain had been small; the loss had been great—the Allies suffered nearly 300,000 casualties over the four months of the battle. Exposure to mustard gas had permanently disabled thousands more.

Canadians were horrified by the news of Passchendaele. Prime Minister Robert Borden visited the troops, crying in private over what he saw. "If this ever happens again," Borden said to the British prime minister, "not a single soldier more will leave our shores."

By the end of 1917, Canadians and the rest of the Allied forces were exhausted, grimly enduring each horrible day at the front. The war had begun in optimism and patriotism, but the longer it went on, the more the ideals of glorious courage and fighting for one's country died, drowning in the mud of the front lines.

For centuries, the countries of Europe had gone to war with each other, fighting over royal successions or territorial boundaries. World War I had started in the same way as all these other wars, but no one was prepared for the devastation new technologies would bring to the battlefield. Machine

No-Man's-Land

guns, poison gas, barbed wire, tanks, submarines, and airplanes all added to the death toll. Trenches crisscrossed the bleak countryside, a result of the development of artillery and machine guns. But trench warfare was slow and inefficient. It was essentially a defensive strategy, and leaving the cover of the trenches for the exposed ground of No-Man's-Land always cost thousands of lives.

At home, Canadians had been just as enthusiastic about the war as the soldiers who left to fight. As the years went by with no noticeable victories on the Western Front in northern France, though, the war seemed increasingly pointless. With the *decimation* of the Allied forces at battles such as the Somme, Vimy Ridge, and Passchendaele, more soldiers were needed to achieve victory over the Germans. Most Allied coun-

The Air War

Airplanes had been used for a decade before the outbreak of World War I, with the first flight by the Wright brothers taking place in 1903. At the beginning of the war, airplanes were used for surveillance and observation. Soon, though, both sides began mounting guns on their aircraft and using planes to drop bombs.

Pilots needed to be skilled at maneuvering their aircraft as well as shooting at other planes. An elite group of fighters emerged, the flying aces, with prestigious awards going to those who had shot down large numbers of enemy planes.

The top flying ace of the war was the Red Baron, the German pilot Manfred von Richthofen, but close behind was the Canadian Billy Bishop. By the end of the war, Bishop had shot down seventy-two enemy planes. Bishop was so popular that the Canadian government began to worry about the blow to morale if he was shot down. In June of 1918, the government ordered him to leave France and go to Britain. Bishop was furious. The morning before he was to leave, he flew out to the enemy lines and destroyed his last five German planes in fifteen minutes.

Bishop was not the only Canadian flying ace, although he was the most famous. Others included Will Barker, the most decorated Canadian war hero; Raymond Collishaw, Canada's second-highest scoring ace; and Roy Brown, who may have shot down the Red Baron.

tries had already started *conscripting* men to serve in the army. Canada, united at the beginning of the war and exhilarated by the Canadian victory at Vimy Ridge, would soon be divided by the issue of conscription.

Conscripting means drafting someone into military service.

World War I introduced air warfare as well as aerial photography.

Three
THE WAR AT HOME

At 8:30 on the evening of February 3, 1916, Canadian prime minister Robert Borden was interrupted in his office at the Parliament buildings in Ottawa when someone banged on the door—and then shouted, "Fire! Fire!"

Borden opened the door to find the hallway filled with smoke. Coughing, he dropped to his knees and started crawling under the smoke toward the exit. He escaped into the cold winter night with minor burns but alive. The center block of the Parliament buildings had been almost completely destroyed, including Borden's office and papers.

Fire in Ottawa's Parliament buildings

*The **cabinet** is a group of advisers to a country's leader.*

__Saboteurs__ are people who purposely destroy or damage equipment, often in times of war.

German detainees at a camp in British Columbia

The next morning, Canadians learned the fire had been started by a cigar left burning in a wastebasket in the Reading Room. Instantly, people thought of sabotage and German spies. A war raged in Europe, and few Canadians doubted the Germans were behind the fire at the Parliament buildings.

Fear and Suspicion

When Canada had gone to war in Europe in 1914, the government had passed the War Measures Act. The act gave the prime minister and his **cabinet** extensive power, bypassing the need to go through Parliament. The War Measures Act was intended as an emergency action to speed up the workings of the government during the unusual circumstances of war. The government had the power to control any part of daily life it thought necessary to help the war effort.

World War I and the War Measures Act had a huge impact on immigrants to Canada, especially those from countries such as Germany, Austria-Hungary, Turkey, or Ukraine (which was then part of the Austro-Hungarian Empire). All immigrants from countries at war with Canada were called "enemy aliens" and were required to register with the government. They had to carry ID cards and were closely watched to make sure they did not plot against Canada and try to overthrow the government from within. These were common practices of many countries during wartime.

During the war, people saw spies and **saboteurs** everywhere, and many did not trust the large communities of immigrants among them. Before long, the Canadian government started to make arrests, rounding up thousands of the

What's in a Name?

Before the war, Berlin, Ontario, was a busy industrial town, known as the German capital of Canada. With the war, and the increasing suspicion of "enemy aliens," the town was viewed with hostility. A bust of the German kaiser Wilhelm set up in the town park was thrown into a nearby lake twice before being destroyed. In 1916, some people tried to have the name of the town changed. Most residents of Berlin did not want the name changed, but this attitude was looked at as suspicious and anti-Canadian. When a referendum on the issue took place in May of 1916, only a few people came out to vote. On September 1 of the same year, Berlin officially became Kitchener, Ontario, named for the late British secretary of war, Lord Kitchener.

Berlin was not the only name change during the war years. Even the king of Britain changed his family name from the German, House of Saxe-Coburg-Gotha, to the very English, House of Windsor.

"enemy aliens" and placing them in camps. By the end of the war, over 8,500 people had been sent to camps; over 5,000 of them were Ukrainians.

Events that would have been considered tragic accidents before the war began were now viewed as suspicious. When the Parliament buildings burned in February of 1916, newspapers across Canada claimed Germans had deliberately set the fire. In September of the same year, a Québec bridge under construction collapsed as the final section was being lowered into place. Immediately, Canadians thought of sabotage, although an investigation soon revealed the accident had been caused by a construction problem.

The Conscription Crisis

As the third year of World War I dragged on, the Allies started to run out of soldiers. Long and terrible battles such as the Somme and Passchendaele had cost hundreds of thousands of men, and the war showed no sign of ending soon. Russia, facing a revolution at home, dropped out of the war in March of 1917, leaving Germany free to concentrate its forces on the Western Front. At the beginning of the war, with patriotism and enthusiasm running high, recruits had been easy to find. By 1917, though, most of those who were willing and able to fight were already on the battlefields of Europe. Britain had begun conscripting soldiers the year before. Prime Minister Robert Borden, after seeing the conditions of the battlefield, knew more men were needed soon to win the war.

Canada had already sent 500,000 men to fight in Europe—one-third the number of eligible Canadian men between the ages of fifteen and forty-nine—but this would not be enough if the war kept on as it was going. In

Posters encouraged Canadians to enlist.

May of 1917, Borden told Parliament that Canada would soon begin a conscription of soldiers, requiring men to serve in the army.

Québec politicians were furious. French Canadians had supported the war in the beginning, but by 1917, the continuing fighting seemed utterly pointless to them. Canadians were dying by the thousands in France for every step of ground gained. To send more men to their deaths for such a senseless war looked like nothing more than insanity.

Many English Canadians supported the idea of conscription. Even though the war was being fought mainly in France, the Canadian war effort was very British. Almost all the Canadian battalions spoke only English, and the soldiers trained in Britain before going to the battlefields. When the House of Commons voted on the proposed Military Service Act, nearly all the English members voted for it, while the French members voted against it. The act passed and went into effect on August 29, 1917.

The Election of 1917

After the outrage caused by the conscription crisis, Borden faced an upcoming general election in December. The first thing Borden did was to form a coalition government, one made up of both Conservative and Liberal politicians. In this way, ideally, political

Poster portraying those left behind

*Those who believe in pacifism, the peaceful resolution of conflicts, are called **pacifists**.*

__Conscientious objectors__ are people who, for moral or religious reasons, believe war is wrong and refuse to serve in any branch of the armed services.

differences would be put aside in order to focus completely on winning the war.

Next, Borden changed the people who were eligible to vote in Canada. No one who had immigrated to Canada within the last fifteen years could vote and neither could *pacifists* and *conscientious objectors*. On the other hand, all soldiers could vote, no matter when they had come to Canada. Also, women were allowed to vote for the first time, as long as they had husbands or relatives fighting in the war. Borden's careful choosing of who could vote and who could not meant the majority of voters would be those likely to approve of conscription.

Paying for War

In 1917, to help meet war expenses, Prime Minister Borden introduced the Income War Tax Act. This income tax was intended to be a temporary measure, only used to build funds needed to pay for the war. Families with children received large exemptions, and only earnings above what was needed for living expenses were taxed. Despite the fact that the tax had been introduced as temporary, it remained in effect after the end of the war. Income tax—with much less generous exemptions—is still around today.

Sheet music stirred up patriotism.

The election was fought between Borden's Union government, a mix of Conservatives and Liberals, and a group of Liberals led by Sir Wilfrid Laurier. Soldiers voting from Europe were simply offered a choice of voting for "government" or "opposition." The Military Voters Act also allowed these soldiers to choose the voting district where they wanted their vote to count. This act let officials encourage soldiers to vote in districts where the government needed the most votes.

The fight between Borden's government and Laurier's anticonscription Liberals was ugly and bitter. When the election results were in, Laurier had won almost all the seats in Québec, and Borden had won almost all the seats in the rest of Canada. Borden remained prime minister, but the cost of introducing conscription had been high. The country was extremely divided, separated along lines of French and English Canada.

The Halifax Explosion

On December 6, 1917, at just before nine in the morning, a French ship, the *Mont Blanc*, collided with a Norwegian cargo ship in the entrance to the Halifax harbor. The *Mont Blanc* was carrying 2,700 tons of explosives headed for the war in Europe. When the two ships ran into each other, sparks from the crash ignited fumes from flammable liquid stored on the deck of the *Mont Blanc*.

In only a few minutes, the ship was ablaze. The sailors flung themselves into the lifeboats, rowing for their lives away from the *Mont Blanc*. The burning ship drifted, heading toward shore.

People gathered to watch the fire, not realizing the danger. The crew of the *Mont Blanc* did not speak English, and no one understood their frantic shouts of warning. Twenty minutes after the two ships had collided, the *Mont Blanc* exploded, flattening a square mile (2.5 square kilometers) of the city of Halifax. Over a thousand people died almost instantly, many of whom had come to the harbor to watch the excitement. Thousands more were seriously injured. Windows were blown out for miles around—as far away as Truro, Nova Scotia, sixty-two miles (100 kilometers) away—and many had eye injuries from flying glass.

The day after the explosion, a blizzard raged through Halifax, paralyzing the rescue and relief efforts. People who had lost their homes and belongings huddled in makeshift shelters or train cars. Within two days, aid began to arrive from the rest of

The Halifax explosion

Canada and from Boston. Doctors worked to treat the injured, developing new and better techniques to deal with eye injuries in the process. Bodies were dug out of rubble, identified if possible, and buried. Temporary housing was built. For months, a massive relief and rebuilding effort took place in Halifax.

Some, of course, blamed foreigners and "enemy aliens" for the explosion. A few believed the Norwegians had actually been Germans who steered their ship toward the explosive-laden *Mont Blanc* on purpose. An initial inquiry found the *Mont Blanc* to be at fault and charged its captain and pilot, along with the commander of the Halifax harbor. A further appeal to the Supreme Court of Canada and the British Privy Council, however, reversed this ruling, giving equal blame to both the Norwegian and French ships. The charges against all three men were thrown out.

Indirectly, the explosion had been caused by the war, since the explosives on the *Mont Blanc* had been headed for the battlefields of Europe. The people of Halifax wanted someone to blame, but the Halifax explosion had been a tragic accident, more a case of bad timing and unfortunate coincidences than of malice or negligence. The horrors of war had come home to Canada in the Halifax explosion.

The Imo, *another ship in the Halifax harbor, was also damaged in the explosion.*

Canada's Hundred Days

Meanwhile, in Europe, the Allies knew they needed to make a major breakthrough on the front line if they were to win the war. The United States had entered the war in 1917, bringing with them needed soldiers to bolster the Allied forces. The arrival of fresh fighting men helped, but since the Americans refused to allow their soldiers to work under the command of British or French officers, their presence was not as effective as it could have been. The Germans pushed deeply into France before their advance faltered. They had moved quickly but had not carried many supplies with them. When they ran short of food, the men rioted, ending the German offensive.

The Germans had been able to make such great gains in so short a time because they had not used trench warfare. During the first three years of the war, trench warfare had been used almost exclusively, and the front line had remained virtually unchanged. Fighting from the trenches led to long battles, extremely high casualty rates, and very little gains. Many battles ended in stalemates or near-stalemates. The war had become one of *attrition*, in which both sides tried to slowly wear the other down with continual losses until they had nothing left with which to fight.

Ferdinand Foch

In order to best retaliate against the Germans, the Allies made the French field marshal, Ferdinand Foch, Supreme Commander of the Allied Forces. Foch could coordinate attacks with strategies using all the Allied soldiers.

The Allies began planning a major offensive against the Germans, and the Canadians were the secret weapon of this plan. At Vimy Ridge and at Passchendaele, they had earned the reputation of being formidable fighters. If the Germans noticed Canadian soldiers gathering in a certain area, they would know where to expect a major attack. To deceive the enemy, several battalions of Canadians traveled to the area around Passchendaele and allowed the Germans to see them there. False radio messages implied the rest of the Canadian forces were massing in the north. Then the Canadians traveled secretly by night further south to the area around Amiens, where the real attack was planned.

The success of the assault depended partly on the element of surprise, and the Germans were surprised. On August 8,

Children playing in World War I trenches

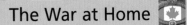

1918, the first day of the Battle of Amiens, the Allies, with Canadians in the forefront, pushed the Germans back eight miles (13 kilometers). The Allies had abandoned trench warfare, fighting from an offensive rather than defensive position.

The last three months of the war became known as Canada's Hundred Days. The Canadians pushed the line of the Western

The end of World War I

Front relentlessly further and further back, leading the Allied forces to victory. They broke through the Hindenburg Line, a barricade of strong German fortifications. They took tens of thousands of prisoners and defeated a quarter of the German army.

The morale of the Germans crumbled. Germany had run short of soldiers and was facing protests and riots against the continuing war. All over the world, people wanted this war to end.

On November 11, 1918, the Germans suddenly surrendered, and at 11:11 in the morning the *armistice* was signed. The German commanders had decided their choice lay between surrender or total destruction. They chose to end the fighting.

World War I was one of the most terrible wars in history, and it changed the world forever. People were no longer so filled with intense feelings of nationalism and imperialism. Their innocent optimism had been destroyed.

Canada faced these changes along with the rest of the world, but the country experienced other changes as well. The skill and success of Canada's soldiers had brought Canada out of the shadow of Britain. A country for fifty years, Canada had at last earned the right to a greater independence from Britain. Even during the middle of the war, the need for this independence began to grow very apparent.

*An **armistice** is a truce in war to discuss terms for reaching a peaceful settlement.*

Civilians celebrate the end of the war.

A postcard commemorating World War I's allies

Four

TOWARD A GREATER INDEPENDENCE

In 1915, Prime Minister Robert Borden visited the Canadian troops in France and traveled to Britain to discuss the war effort with the British Parliament. Even though Borden was the leader of a country that had sent over 100,000 soldiers to fight, no one would share information with him. "Canada deserves to have access to information about the war and to be consulted in matters concerning us," he told the British.

"Not possible," the *colonial secretary* replied, and Borden went back to Canada dissatisfied and disgusted. In a letter dated January 4, 1916, Borden poured out his frustrations to one of his *cabinet* members serving in London:

> [I have received] just what information could be gleaned from the daily press and no more . . . steps of the most important and even vital character have been taken, postponed or rejected without the slightest consultation with the authorities of this Dominion. It can hardly be expected that we shall put 400,000 or 500,000 men in the field and willingly accept the position of having no more voice and receiving no more consideration than if we were toy *automata*.

A *colonial secretary* was the official in charge of affairs to do with British colonies.

A *cabinet* is a group of advisers.

Automata are relatively self-operating machines.

*If a country is **autonomous**, it is politically independent and self-governing.*

*A **commonwealth** is an association of Britain and sovereign states.*

Imperial War Conference

In December of 1916, David Lloyd George became prime minister of Great Britain. Lloyd George was much more willing to work with Canada and Britain's other former colonies than his predecessor. In March of 1917, Lloyd George called an Imperial War Conference. Instead of treating the Dominions—Canada, Newfoundland, Australia, New Zealand, and South Africa—as though they were merely a part of Britain, Lloyd George invited the leaders of those

David Lloyd George

countries to take part in the conference. The idea was to give the Dominions a chance to participate in the discussions concerning the direction the war would take, although Britain would still make the final decisions.

At the conference, Borden presented Resolution IX, which he had written himself. The resolution stated that the Dominions were "*autonomous* nations of an Imperial *commonwealth*" and had a right "to an adequate voice in foreign policy and foreign relations." Jan Smuts, of the South African delegation, seconded the proposed resolution. The conference delegates put Borden's proposed resolution to a vote, and Resolution IX was passed.

The structure of the political world was beginning to change. No longer would former British colonies, such as Canada or Australia, be a part of the British Empire. Resolution IX was one of the first steps toward the development of a commonwealth of nations. In such a commonwealth, the Dominions would be fully independent countries on an equal status with Britain.

Paris Peace Conference

After the end of the war, Canada participated in the Paris Peace Conference, a yearlong series of meetings to negotiate treaties with the former enemies of the Allied forces. The first of these treaties was the Treaty of Versailles, signed on June 28, 1919, an agreement with Germany that officially ended the war.

Normally, Britain would have signed for Canada and the other Dominions, but Robert Borden wanted the world to see that Canada and the other former British colonies spoke for themselves and made their own decisions about foreign policy and diplomatic affairs. Borden read the entire treaty carefully and then signed his own name. Each of the Dominion delegates did the same.

Canada's attendance at the Paris Peace Conference and the signatures of the Canadian delegates on the Treaty of Versailles made no official difference to Canada's status as a country independent of Britain. These things were symbolic acts, showing that Canada was taking a greater responsibility in international events.

The League of Nations

At the Paris Peace Conference, the delegates decided to create a League of Nations to try to prevent the outbreak of another world war. The League would be made up of members from most of the countries that

The Paris Peace Conference was shaped by these four leaders: David Lloyd George of England, Vittorio Orlando of Italy, Georges Clemenceau of France, and Woodrow Wilson of the United States.

had fought with the Allies in the First World War, as well as from neutral countries. The League's purpose would be to negotiate disagreements between countries and to improve conditions all over the world.

Woodrow Wilson, president of the United States, had pushed to have the creation of the League of Nations included in the Treaty of Versailles. When the delegates of the Paris Peace Conference signed the Treaty of Versailles, they agreed to create a League of Nations.

Although the idea of forming a League of Nations had been put forward at the Paris Peace Conference by the American president, the Americans chose not to join it themselves. One reason the Americans did not want to join was that they wanted to free themselves from world politics and go back to their *isolationist* policies. The United States had entered the war reluctantly—only after Germany had reinstated a policy of attacking American merchant ships with submarines early in 1917.

Another reason the United States did not want to join the League of Nations was that they did not approve of Canada and the other Dominions being allowed to join as full members. They believed the Dominions were simply extensions of Britain and that therefore Britain would have several votes instead of just one.

Despite Americans' doubts, joining the League of Nations was another triumph for Canadian independence and nationalism. For the first time, Canada was looked on as an equal among nations, a respected member of the global community.

The League of Nations met for the first time on January 10, 1920. The organization lasted until the outbreak of World War II, but it had serious internal problems, even before then. The

*If a country is **isolationist**, it avoids international relations in favor of national interests.*

Woodrow Wilson

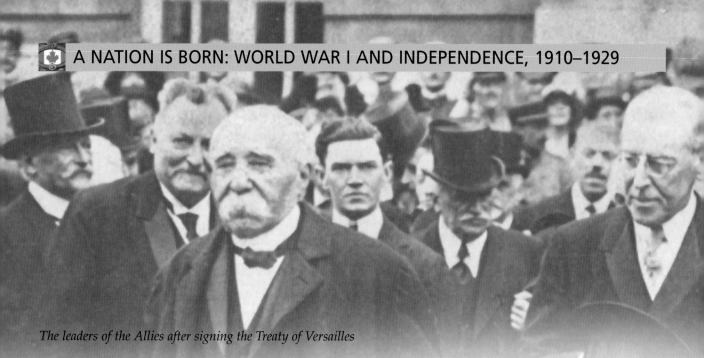

The leaders of the Allies after signing the Treaty of Versailles

fact that the United States refused to join meant not all the major world powers took part. The League had good intentions for creating a world community, but the member nations were still much more concerned with looking after their own national interests than they were in global issues. Another major problem was that all of the members had to approve each decision, a nearly impossible task. After World War II, and the League's failure to prevent it, the United Nations was created in place of the League of Nations.

The First World War had brought Canada a greater role in world politics. From the respect earned by Canadian troops on the battlefields to the symbolic Canadian signing of the Treaty of Versailles to Canada's membership in the League of Nations, the war had resulted in a greater independence for Canada. No longer would Canada be thought of as simply another former British colony.

As Canada earned its independence internationally, the war had brought more changes at home. Women had been given greater freedoms during the war years than they had ever known before. Workers had been pushed to their limits by the demand for goods needed to fight the war. With the war over, both these groups wanted more freedoms, a greater voice in their own destinies.

Covenant of the League of Nations

The High Contracting Parties, in order to promote international co-operation and to achieve international peace and security by the acceptance of obligations not to resort to war, by the prescription of open, just and honourable relations between nations, by the firm establishment of the understandings of international law as the actual rule of conduct among Governments, and by the maintenance of justice and a scrupulous respect for all treaty obligations in the dealings of organised peoples with one another, Agree to this Covenant of the League of Nations.

Canadian soldiers returning from the battlefield

Five
THE NEED FOR SOCIAL FREEDOM

The young soldiers, exhausted by war, returned home to Canada by the shipload. They had left with dreams of glory, but now they wanted nothing more than to get married, find a job, and settle down peacefully for the rest of their lives. But where were the jobs? During the war, factories had churned out airplanes, weapons, and uniforms to send overseas, but the need for those things ended with the war. Now, Canadian soldiers found themselves accepting low-paying jobs, often in difficult factory conditions. Many joined labor unions in an effort to fight for a better working life.

Labor Unions

With the beginning of the *industrial revolution* in the late eighteenth century, workers had started organizing themselves into labor unions, groups of workers, usually for a specific trade, who joined together to try to gain higher wages and better working conditions.

The war brought many jobs, more jobs than workers in fact. Since manufacturers needed to attract workers, the em-

*The term **industrial revolution** refers to the social and economic changes that began in the late eighteenth century and involved the widespread adoption of industrial production methods.*

Socialism is a political theory or system in which the means of production and distribution are controlled by the people and operated according to fairness, not market principles.

Aristocracy refers to people of the highest social classes.

Karl Marx

66

Newsletter distributed by the One Big Union

ployees were able to demand higher pay and better conditions. Despite this, the war meant everything cost more, so workers did not really have any more money.

When the war ended, so did the need for high numbers of employees. The way work was done had changed as well. In the past, labor had often been done by individuals, but the beginning of the twentieth century brought large factories and assembly-line work. No longer did workers need to be highly skilled. Skilled craftspeople, who needed a lot of training, had once made more money. Now these workers worried they would lose their jobs to lower-paid employees who could do the work with few specialized skills.

Unions had been around for a long time by World War I, but new ideas, such as *socialism*, had begun to take root. In 1867, Karl Marx published *Das Kapital*, describing how workers did all the work while the business owners got rich. People read Marx's book and agreed. In 1917, workers in Russia, led by Vladimir Lenin, a follower of Marxism, rebelled against the wealthy upper class. They overthrew the *aristocracy* and killed the tsar and his family.

After the war, immigrants to Canada and returning soldiers brought with them Marxist ideas. Although many Canadians

Manitoba

WINNIPEG,

ONE KILLED, SCO
FOLLOWING AN AT

ob Attacked Mounted Police Who
Were Forced to Fire — Riot Act Read

PROC

Radical means favoring vast, quick, and often violent change from current practices or beliefs.

Conservative means a dislike of change, favoring instead the status quo.

Newspaper account of the violence in Winnipeg

had belonged to labor unions for years, new unions were formed, more *radical* and revolutionary than the unions of the past.

Labor unions before the war had usually consisted of small groups of a certain type of worker. After the war, people tried to organize larger, more inclusive unions, formed of all workers. These large unions sometimes wanted to push not only for changes in employee wages and conditions, but for sweeping political changes, as had happened in Russia.

One such union in Canada was the One Big Union (OBU), so named because it wanted to take in all other unions. The OBU was formed in the spring of 1919, after many workers became frustrated with the *conservative* methods of the

ree Press

, JUNE 21, 1919

ES HURT IN RIOT
EMPT TO PARADE

CYCLONE SWEEPS FERGUS FALLS; HUNDREDS DIE

Five Killed When Tram Hits Quebec Auto Party

GERMANS VOTE TO SIGN PEACE TREATY TERMS

Trades and Labour Congress, the group overseeing labor concerns and unions in Canada. The OBU wanted quick reforms for workers. Their demands included a six-hour workday and a five-day workweek, higher wages, and legal status for the OBU.

The Winnipeg General Strike

Workers had long used striking as a way to make employers listen to their complaints. Striking employees would refuse to work,

hoping to force company owners to meet their demands. More radical unions in the early twentieth century, such as the OBU, promoted general strikes, in which all the workers in a certain town or city would stop work at once.

In 1918, city workers in Winnipeg, Manitoba, had gone on strike, and across the city union members joined them in sympathy strikes. The Winnipeg government, unsure how to handle such a widespread strike, had quickly given in to the workers' demands.

Anarchists are people who reject the need for a government.

A year later, labor conditions in Canada had deteriorated. The war was over, and jobs were no longer as plentiful. This made employers slower to give in to demands. In the spring of 1919, machinists at a Winnipeg shop tried to form a union, but the company refused, and the machinists walked off their jobs in a strike. Hearing about the case, several Winnipeg unions joined the strike in a show of sympathy.

Workers wanted change. They had seen in 1918 how a general strike could give the workers power. On May 15, at eleven in the morning, a citywide general strike began.

The Great Influenza Pandemic

In 1918, a flu epidemic broke out across the world, more deadly than any other in history. The epidemic began in March and lasted for a year and a half. Soldiers were among the hardest hit, and they carried the disease with them as they returned home after the war. Around the world, over twenty million people died of the flu, with some estimates running as high as a hundred million.

In Canada, 50,000 died. Some small towns were completely wiped out. Unlike most flu outbreaks, which killed the youngest and oldest, many of those who died in the 1918–1919 pandemic were between twenty and forty years old.

The general strike

called the strikers **anarchists** and portrayed them as vicious fanatics and revolutionaries. In reality, the strikers were generally peaceful. They believed their actions would bring changes for the better, and as a result, they were happy and excited to be involved.

To deal with the strike, a Citizens' Committee of One Thousand formed in Winnipeg, made up of company owners and politicians. The committee wanted to call in the army to arrest the strikers, but this was illegal. To end the strike, the Canadian minister of justice, Arthur Meighen, introduced a law under which people could be arrested if they were suspected of promoting revolution.

On June 17, the new law was used to arrest the leaders of the Winnipeg strike and throw them into prison. Angry at these unfair arrests, on Saturday, June 21, the striking workers gathered outside City Hall to protest. The mayor called out the police to break up the crowd, and a riot began. Hundreds of "special police," created to deal with the strike, arrived, armed with clubs. The police fired into the crowd, killing one man and injuring several more. The crowd scattered, but people found their way blocked by the club-wielding "specials." Thirty were injured and more than eighty arrested by the time the riot ended.

Almost all the Winnipeg unions joined the strike, along with thousands of nonunionized workers. Over 30,000 people stopped working in Winnipeg, effectively shutting down the city. Across the country, as unions heard about the Winnipeg strike, they called sympathy strikes to show their support.

The Winnipeg strike, along with the sympathy strikes it generated across Canada, worried the government. Officials feared the strikes would lead to the kind of radical violence seen in Russia in 1917. Newspapers

Suffrage *means the right to vote.*

A play, story, or other work of art that is **satirical** *exposes some aspect of human behavior to ridicule and scorn.*

Four days later, strike leaders, fearing a repeat of "Bloody Saturday," called off the strike.

The violent end of the Winnipeg strike shocked workers. After that, Canadians were slower to try striking as a solution to labor problems. On the other hand, the Liberal Party, concerned about an increase in revolutionary uprisings, promised to bring labor reforms.

Women's suffrage political cartoon

Votes for Women

The woman's movement had been around for over a century by the early twentieth century, although for years the gains made by women were slow and gradual. Many men denied that women could possibly be equal to men. Most women were not allowed to vote. In Canada, the move toward women's *suffrage* began in Manitoba.

In 1914, Nellie McClung, a popular writer and speaker from Winnipeg, put on a *satirical* play called *The Women's Parliament*. In it, the roles of men and women were reversed, with women in leadership positions and men petitioning to gain the vote. McClung played the role of the premier, imitating Manitoba's conservative leader, Rodman Roblin.

The day before the performance, McClung and a delegation of women had approached Roblin to ask that women be granted the right to vote. Roblin replied, with a condescending little laugh, that:

Nellie McClung

Any civilization which has produced the noble women I see before me is good enough for me. . . . Gentle woman, queen of the home, set apart by her great function of motherhood. . . . And you say women are the equal of men? I tell you you are wrong. . . . Women are superior to men, now and always!

Many men believed, as Roblin did, that respectable women would not want to vote. Women, they thought, were fragile and beautiful creatures to be protected by men. Women could not understand political issues because their minds were not made that way. Allowing women to vote would only cause upheaval in the home.

Nellie McClung, acting in the satirical *The Women's Parliament*, used Roblin's words and gestures as she spoke about how "Men were made to support families. Why," McClung exclaimed, "if men start to vote, they will vote too much. Politics unsettles men, and unsettled men mean unsettled bills, broken furniture, broken vows, and divorce."

The audience, composed of both men and women, loved the play. The move for women's suffrage began to take hold in western Canada, and in January of 1916, the newly elected Liberal government of Manitoba gave women the right to vote in provincial elections. Later that same year, Saskatchewan and Alberta gave women the same rights, with British Columbia and Ontario following in 1917. By the end of the 1920s, all the Canadian provinces had granted women's suffrage except for Québec, which would not give women the vote until 1940.

In 1917, Prime Minister Robert Borden granted some women the right to vote in the federal election on a limited basis. The next year, suffrage was extended to all white Canadian women—women and men of other ethnic backgrounds would take longer to gain the right to vote.

The Persons Case

After women had gained the vote, some of the leaders of the women's movement ran for political offices. In 1921, Nellie McClung became a member of the Alberta legislature for the Edmonton district. In the same year, Agnes Campbell Macphail became the first woman to be elected as a Member of Parliament in the federal government.

Although women could now legitimately run for federal offices, they could not be appointed to the Senate. The British North America Act of 1867, which had created the country of Canada and laid out the structure of the Canadian government, stated that only "persons" could be appointed to the Senate. The word "persons" had always been interpreted to mean men, not women.

In 1927, five women—known as the Famous Five—challenged the assumed definition of the word "persons." They appealed to the Supreme Court of Canada, asking the question, "Does the word 'person' include women?" These women, led by Emily Murphy, the first female magistrate in Canada, were all at the forefront of the Canadian women's movement, and many of them were involved in politics. The other members of the Famous Five were Nellie

Agnes Campbell Macphail

Cairine Wilson, first woman senator

McClung; Irene Parlby, a provincial cabinet minister from Alberta; Louise McKinney, a former member of the Alberta legislature; and Henrietta Muir Edwards, the cofounder of the National Council of Women.

On April 24, 1928, the Supreme Court handed down its ruling. Women were not persons. One court ruled above the Supreme Court, the British Privy Council. The Famous Five took the case to the Privy Council and presented them with the same question.

Lord Chancellor Sankey of the Privy Council read the verdict on October 18, 1929. This time, the Famous Five got the answer they were looking for. "The exclusion of women from all public offices is a relic of days more barbarous than ours," Sankey said.

In 1930, Cairine Wilson was the first woman appointed to the Canadian Senate. Wilson went on to become the first woman delegate to the UN General Assembly in 1949 and the first woman deputy speaker in 1955.

Women's Work

Women like Nellie McClung and Emily Murphy worked for years to gain the attention of politicians. They were often viewed as "unladylike" and considered dangerous disrupters. For years, men had been arguing that "woman's place is in the home."

When World War I began, not enough men remained to fill the jobs. Suddenly, women were needed to grow crops and work in factories. Most men believed this was a temporary necessity, a sacrifice needed to win the war. During the war, however, women proved they were just as capable as men.

Emily Murphy

With the war over, jobs became scarce. Women were no longer needed in many jobs. Returning soldiers expected their wives to go back to the way they were be-

Workers' union poster

Gradually, the way people looked at working women began to change. After the war, people started believing it was acceptable for women to work in some jobs, at least until they were married. Jobs such as nursing or telephone operator work were seen as perfectly acceptable for women (and therefore not acceptable for men).

The early part of the twentieth century was a time of social upheaval in Canada, as it was in many parts of the world. Workers began organizing into large unions, while women petitioned to gain the right to vote and to be treated as equals to men. Both labor reforms and greater freedoms for women would continue to be gained throughout the twentieth century.

In the next decades, Canada and the world around it would face more crises. The Great Depression would create widespread poverty and economic concerns. Then, another world war would begin, born out of the First World War and the financial hardships that followed in Germany. Canada would again fight with the world and would once more be forced to deal with the issue of conscription.

fore the war, staying at home and looking after the children. Women were often not satisfied to be suddenly denied the freedoms they had discovered during wartime.

May 4, 1910 Naval Service of Canada is officially created; name is changed to Royal Canadian Navy in 1911.

1867 Britain passes the British North America Act, creating the country of Canada.

October 1914 Canadian Expeditionary Force leaves Canada for basic training in Great Britain.

June 1914 Archduke Franz Ferdinand, heir to the throne of Austria-Hungary, and his wife, Sophie, are assassinated in Sarajevo.

1899 The Boer War begins; it ends in 1902.

April 22, 1915 Germany introduces chlorine gas as a new weapon.

January 1916 The Liberal government of Manitoba gives women the right to vote in provincial elections.

April 1915 Canadian forces take part in their first major battle, the Second Battle of Ypres.

July 1915 Germany introduces mustard gas as a weapon.

February 3, 1916 Parliament buildings in Ottawa burn.

December 6, 1917 The Halifax explosion occurs when the *Mont Blanc* collides with a Norwegian cargo ship in the entrance to the Halifax harbor.

1917 Prime Minister Borden introduces the Income War Tax Act.

May 1917 Canada starts conscription.

November 11, 1918 The Germans suddenly surrender and the armistice is signed.

1917 Prime Minister Robert Borden grants some women the right to vote in the federal election on a limited basis; the next year, suffrage is extended to all white Canadian women.

1919 The One Big Union is formed.

January 10, 1920 League of Nations meets for the first time.

June 28, 1919 Treaty of Versailles is signed, officially ending World War I.

1927 The Famous Five challenge the assumed definition of the word "person."

1930 Cairine Wilson becomes the first woman appointed to the Canadian Senate.

FURTHER READING

Baker, David. *William Avery "Billy" Bishop: The Man and the Aircraft He Flew*. Los Angeles: Books Nippan, 1991.

Benham, Mary Lile. *Nellie McClung*. Markham, Ont.: Fitzhenry & Whiteside, 2000.

Bumstead, J. M. *Winnipeg General Strike of 1919: An Illustrated History*. Winnipeg, Man.: J. Gordon Shillingford Publishing, 1996.

Fraser, Donald. *The Journal of Private Fraser: Canadian Expeditionary Force, 1914–1918*. Ottawa, Ont.: CEF Books, 2002.

Glasner, Joyce. *The Halifax Explosion: Surviving the Blast that Shook a Nation*. Canmore, Alb.: Altitude Publishing, 2003.

Millar, Nancy. *The Famous Five: Five Canadian Women and Their Fight to Become Persons*. Calgary, Alb.: Deadwood Publishing, 2003.

Ostrower, Gary B. *League of Nations 1919*. Wayne, N.J.: Avery Publishing Group, 1996.

Robson, Pam. *All About the First World War, 1914–18*. London: Hodder Wayland, 2003.

Spigelman, Martin. *Wilfrid Laurier*. Markham, Ont.: Fitzhenry & Whiteside, 2000.

Turner, I. A. J. *Vimy Ridge, 1917: Byng's Canadians Triumph at Arras*. University Park, Ill.: Osprey Publishing, 2005.

FOR MORE INFORMATION

Canada and the First World War
www.collectionscanada.ca/firstworldwar/
index-e.html

Canadian Labor History
www.civilization.ca/hist/labour/
lab01e.html

The Famous Five
www.collectionscanada.ca/famous5/
index-e.html

Imperial Adventure: Canada
and the Boer War
www.civilization.ca/cwm/saw/
index_e.html

In Flanders Fields Museum
www.inflandersfields.be/default2.htm

Newfoundland and the Great War
collections.ic.gc.ca/great_war/home.html

Sir Robert Laird Borden
www.collectionscanada.ca/
primeministers/h4-3200-e.html

Sir Wilfrid Laurier
www.collectionscanada.ca/
primeministers/h4-3175-e.html

The Suffrage Movement
timelinks.merlin.mb.ca/referenc/
db0007.htm

Veteran's Affairs Canada:
The First World War
www.vacacc.gc.ca/general/
sub.cfm?source=history/firstwar

Publisher's note:
The Web sites listed on this page were active at the time of publication. The publisher is not responsible for Web sites that have changed their addresses or discontinued operation since the date of publication. The publisher will review and update the Web-site list upon each reprint.

INDEX

air warfare 38, 39

Battle of Amiens 52–53
Battle of the Somme 28, 30–32
Boer War 11, 13–14, 21
Borden, Robert 20, 21, 36, 41, 44, 45–46, 48,
  57, 59, 74
Bourassi, Henri 13–14, 16
British North America Act 9, 11

Canada's Hundred Days 51–53, 55
Canadian Expeditionary Force 32–33
Canadian navy 14, 16, 18, 21
conscription 39, 44–45, 46, 48

election of 1911 18–19, 21
election of 1917 45–46, 48

Famous Five 75–76
Ferdinand, Archduke Franz 23–24
free trade with the United States 18

gold 11
government 18

Halifax explosion 48–49

Imperial Defence Conference 14
Imperial War Conference 58–59
imperialism 13–14, 16, 21
Income War Tax Act 46
industrial revolution 65

labor unions 65, 67–68
Laurie, Sir Wilfrid 9, 13–14, 16, 17, 18, 21, 48
League of Nations 59–63
Lloyd George, David 58

Marx, Karl 66, 67
McClung, Nellie 73–74
McCrae, Major John 26
Military Service Act 45

nationalism 9, 13–14, 16, 21

One Big Union (OBU) 67, 68

Paris Peace Conference 59, 60–61
Passchendaele 34, 35–37

Royal Canadian Navy 16

socialism 67

Treaty of Versailles 59, 61, 62

United Nations 62

Vimy Ridge 32–34, 39

War Measures Act 42
Wilson, Woodrow 60, 61

Winnipeg General Strike 69–72
women's suffrage 72, 73
World War I 21, 56

Ypres 25

PICTURE CREDITS

Canada Fisheries and Oceans: p. 15

Canadian Department of Foreign Affairs and International Trade: p. 20

Canadian Veteran's Affairs: pp. 64–65

Canadian War Museum: p. 44

Corel: p. 19

First World War.com: pp. 30–31, 49, 52–53

National Archives of Canada: pp. 23, 40–41, 42, 73, 75, 78–79

NOAA: p. 39

Photos.com: pp. 8–9, 12, 27

Provincial Archives of Manitoba: p. 67

Public Archives of Nova Scotia: p. 50

Saskatchewan Archives: p. 33

BIOGRAPHIES

Sheila Nelson was born in Newfoundland and grew up in both Newfoundland and Ontario. She has written a number of history books for kids and always enjoys the chance to keep learning. She recently earned a master's degree and now lives in Rochester, New York, with her husband and daughter.

SERIES CONSULTANT

Dr. David Bercuson is the Director of the Centre for Military and Strategic Studies at the University of Calgary. His writings on modern Canadian politics, Canadian defense and foreign policy, and Canadian military, among other topics, have appeared in academic and popular publications. Dr. Bercuson is the author, coauthor, or editor of more than thirty books, including *Confrontation at Winnipeg: Labour, Industrial Relations, and the General Strike* (1990), *Colonies: Canada to 1867* (1992), *Maple Leaf Against the Axis, Canada's Second World War* (1995), and *Christmas in Washington: Roosevelt and Churchill Forge the Alliance* (2005). He has also served as historical consultant for several film and television projects, and provided political commentary for CBC radio and television and CTV television. In 1989, Dr. Bercuson was elected a fellow of the Royal Society of Canada. In 2004, Dr. Bercuson received the Vimy Award, sponsored by the Conference of Defence Association Institute, in recognition of his significant contributions to Canada's defense and the preservation of the Canadian democratic principles.